AF432605

SECRETS OF A SUGAR BABY

SUGAR BABY SECRETS BOOK 1

MIA BLACK

Copyright © 2019 Mia Black

All rights reserved. This book or any portion thereof may not be reproduced or used in any manner whatsoever without the express written permission of the publisher

PROLOGUE

The streets of D.C. weren't that kind to girls like me and my sister. Despite living in the most powerful place in the most powerful country in the world, we weren't afforded the same luxuries as those we elected to rule over us. As you ventured further out of the capitol, past the Washington Monument, the Mall and the White House, you saw people suffering in despair, their cries being unheard. Poverty affected all races, everybody. We knew where we stood and we did our best to navigate. We were a little bit different from the others. My dad worked for the Treasury and my mom worked for the State Department. They were good jobs, but not enough to live within the gilded gates. We also had family who had fallen victim to the war on drugs, whether it was jail time or to the pipe. It kept us in perspective. It never let us forget that we were black. Unapologetically so.

My sister, Angie, and I. We were grounded. We walked to and from school every day. Only time we had any reprieve, was when it was snowing. However, during the high heat of the summer, we were sweating our presses out as we walked down K Street towards our home. As we got older, our conversations began to change. We went from which Bratz dolls we wanted to which boys Angie liked nowadays. It was as if it was a new boy every week. It was starting to get hard to keep track. I wondered if I would ever be like Angie. She was two years older than me and absolutely stunning.

Angelica Robinson was brown skinned and built to the Gawds. She started blossoming when she was around my age. It was as if it happened overnight. Her hips rounded out, her breasts were large and bouncy and her ass began to barely fit her jeans. Through all of this, her waist remained tiny and flat. I saw the attention it got her. Some good but mostly bad. I watched as older men drooled over her, approaching her even. She sometimes found it amusing and would lead them on. Other times, she would just ignore them. Luckily, I walked with her sometimes, because if not, I don't know if she would make it home at times.

Me, I was about 5'3 and not showing anything. I was just skinny and kind of tall. I didn't know what to do with it. All I knew was that the boys didn't notice me. I didn't think they would ever notice me. We both wore our long brown curls, thanks to some Indian on our mom's side, in long braids that looked like ropes down our back. For the hot May day as we walked back home from school, I twisted mine up into a bun. As we rounded the corner towards our parents' brownstone, we walked past our neighbor Darryl's house. Angie then turned to me and smiled, her eyes darkening. That Cheshire cat smile. She was about to start talking shit. Again.

"So.... When are you guys going to finally do it?"

"Do what?" I asked.

"It... You know what I mean. You know he likes you. The way he stares at you." Angie teased.

"Whatever! You're the one with all the boys, Angie."

She laughed. "Men, honey." She said, "Darryl is a boy and perfect for you. The killing part is, you like him too. You guys should come off of it and be together."

I pushed her slightly and she laughed. "That's how I know."

Darryl was just my friend. That was it. That was all. I didn't know what look she was talking about. All we did all day was talk about videogames and comic books. I didn't really have too many people I could talk to about that. I just shook my head.

"He's just my friend, Angie. Nothing else. How many times do I have to say that?"

"Until I believe you, which I won't," she said to me, laughing. I just wanted to smack her in the face. I hated when she would tease me like that. I just bit down on the inner part of my cheek and kept walking. The last time she was teasing me about Darryl, she ran up to his house and was about to ring his doorbell. I took off running to our house. I then proceeded to get her in trouble by telling our parents about how she ditched school earlier that day. She never attempted to do that again. I made my way, red-faced, to the house. I stopped short of the house and Angie bumped into me.

The door was open. Wide open. I was afraid to go inside. It was too early for this. Way too early. This was the second time we were robbed. I completely hated DC sometimes. Angie still stood behind me, her hands on my shoulders. They left the door open the last time we were robbed which was literally a couple days ago. It was later at night so no one could see what they were doing. We didn't enter the house until the cops arrived and took fingerprints. We were thankful that we were out for back to school night. We didn't know what would have happened if we had actually been home. Burglars in our neighborhood were known to light up the whole family, or at least rape and beat them down. No one was home this early anyway, so we had nothing to worry about regarding family. It would just be the robbers, potentially. I turned to Angie.

"Do you think we should just go inside or should we call the cops?" I asked her.

"I don't think we should call the cops. Maybe when mom and dad get home. I want to go inside and see if everything is okay though. I know that we locked up. Right?"

"Yes, we did." I responded, "We weren't the last ones to leave the house. Mom was still here when we left.

"Let's call mom first and let her know what happened." Angie said. She took out her iPhone and dialed mom. She put the phone to her ear. We thought we heard the ringing in the house but chose to ignore it. Mom would be at work right now. She wouldn't be getting off until roughly five thirty. She hung up the phone and dialed again. We heard the same ringtone go off. Her phone was in the house. Maybe she left it while she was on the way to work. Angie must have read my mind.

"I'll try calling her job," she said and dialed the phone. After holding it to her ear for a few seconds, she put the phone down and shook her head.

"She's not answering." She looked back up at the open door and then dialed again. Mom's cell phone went off. She kept the phone in her hand as she walked to the front door. I pulled out one of my books. I would use that as a weapon, I thought to myself, as I walked behind her. We entered the house slowly, looking around us. We didn't hear any rustling or anything like that. Just the constant ringing of our mother's phone, which we found lying on the table near the door. She didn't come to answer it. Angie finally hung up her phone and looked around. She scratched her head in confusion as she turned to face me.

"This is weird. I don't see anything missing. I mean we didn't have much to take since a couple of days ago, but mom's phone is still here. This doesn't feel right, Jae."

I swallowed past the lump in my throat and nodded my head in agreement.

"Follow me to the kitchen," Angie said as she walked past the foyer. I sighed and reached around to open up my backpack. As I was placing my book back into my backpack, I heard Angie scream at the top of her lungs. I dropped my backpack and ran into the kitchen.

And there she was.

My mother.

My beautiful mother, lying on the kitchen floor, covered in blood. Her throat slashed. Dead.

My mother was dead.

Mymotherwasdead. Mymotherwasdead.

Angie leaned over and placed her hand against the counter. She then threw up everywhere. The smell of her vomit and my mother's blood overcame me. Before the day turned into night, and my legs betrayed my body, I looked into my mother's brown eyes. They were cold, hard and lifeless. That was the last memory I would have of my mother. The world blacked out as my head hit the tile. I hoped that I would join her soon.

I woke up in my bed at my aunt's house. It was all

just a dream, I told myself. A fucking nightmare. My mother was alive, my father was here and it was just a dream. But this nightmare has lasted for four years. I always woke up in this bed, reaching for my mother, but it had been four years since that fateful day and nothing had been right since. I didn't know what I did in a past life to deserve what happened to me. No one should go through this. Ever. That night, I woke up in the hospital with a concussion and little memory of what happened. All I remembered was my mother was dead on the kitchen floor. My father was in the room with me, as was Angie, who just sat in the chair and stared outside the window, looking at the street below.

I was released from the hospital and was told that my mother had died and that we would be moving away as soon as everything was settled. They ruled my mother's death a homicide but they couldn't find a motive other than robbery. The police took into account that our home was robbed a few days before and that they may have come back to finish the job. My mother was just an unfortunate casualty. I never saw my dad cry once. Just like the strong Jamaican men before him, he kept his head up and did his best to take care of his family. My mother wanted to be cremated, so on a muggy D.C.

morning, we scattered my mother's ashes across the Potomac River.

My dad kept Angie and I home for a couple weeks, picking up our school work so we could keep up. As the norm with black folks, he didn't believe in sending us to therapy, but instead kept us in the church week after week. As I would sit there in the pews, looking up at the good white Jesus, I would wonder where God was in my mother's last moments. Where was God in my life?

I struggled to hold on, but He was nowhere to be found. I remembered the day completely that I knew God had left us. My father dropped us off at our Auntie Jeanie's house. The one with no kids, because she lost them all. The one whom... my father wouldn't even allow at my mother's funeral. But she was the only family that he had outside of Jamaica. They came here together when they were eighteen years old and then went on two very different paths. My father went to school and worked for the government, while my auntie got mixed up with the wrong types of dudes and ended up on the government. We had limited contact with her when my mom was alive. She felt like she wasn't a good look to be around. My auntie hated her because my father married a black American woman instead of a JA woman. They were never able to get over it. Now she had no choice.

There we were, in front of her door, in the projects. My father knocked on the door. We waited for a moment as Jeanie walked up to the door and opened it slowly. She leaned against the door jamb and took a long drag on her joint before. She looked us up and down as she blew out the smoke. My father just stared at her and shook his head.

"What ya want?" she asked in her thick accent.

My father reverted back to the tongue of his mother country. "Me want ya watch me guls. Me av' a place a go where they nah go?"

"How long will dat be?"

"Only one night. Me ya be back on morrow."

She gave us the once over one more time and then pushed the door open, motioning for us to come in. We walked inside. The place was cluttered, with clothes and other items everywhere. Angie and I found the only clean place on the couch and sat down, staring at the wall. My father just stared at us as if he was trying to memorize our faces. He then looked at his sister and stared at her before walking out of the doorway, without saying goodbye. I didn't know how to react at that moment. I felt a strange sensation in my heart, like someone was squeezing it. I knew that moment was the last time I would ever see my dad again. I tried to shake it out of my head as my aunt closed the door. Since there was nowhere else to sleep, Angie and I knocked out on the couch. I didn't dream that night.

My fears were confirmed in the morning. We woke up to my aunt cussing in patois as she stood outside the door. We got up and walked towards her. Outside the door was four bags; our dad must've dropped off the rest of our stuff from the house. We no longer had a mother or a father now. Our belongings being left on the porch sealed everything. Aunt Jeanie blew out some smoke and looked down at the bags. She then looked back up at us.

"Well, me guess you a stay with me now. I no got no room for you. You av' ta stay on di couch." She then walked back into the house.

"Get your stuff and close the door." She then walked into the kitchen. I turned to Angie, to look for an answer, anything that would explain what would now be our life. One single tear escaped from her eye. She bit her lower lip and leaned down, picking up her two bags. I swallowed back a lump in my throat as I also picked up my two bags. I shut the door behind me.

The only solace that we had was school. Luckily my aunt still lived in the same area where we could attend. She didn't drop us off or anything, so we had to find our own way around. The kids at school tried their best to avoid talking about what happened to my mother. We tried to keep up the front that my father was still taking care of us but all that changed when my aunt started getting food stamps and welfare for us. We never saw a dime of it. Luckily, we went to a school where we wore uniforms, otherwise we would've got clowned. We would eventually grow out of our clothes and then we would be forced to take measures into our own hands.

Life with Jeanie was rough. I refused to call her auntie because that was a sign of respect. And frankly she didn't deserve any. Over the months, I realized why my dad kept us away for so long. My mom didn't have any siblings on the east coast, so I guess he had to do what he had to do. I guess he thought this was better than the system for his two girls. However, the bitch was legit crazy. The bitch stayed lit off of drugs and alcohol. I wondered how she could afford to stay high and drunk all day until I realized that Melvin was her supplier. He gave her drugs, she paid him with pussy. That should've been enough, or so I thought.

One time, when he thought I was sleep, I felt a hand go

up my skirt and tried to find its way into my underwear. When he couldn't get underneath to touch me, he pressed his fingers, rubbing against me. I tried to pretend I was sleep, trying not to move, until I felt him lift up my shirt and try to pull down my little training bra. Just as he was about to lean over, I jumped up and screamed. He backed off of me and ran out of the room. I covered myself up with a blanket and sat there, shaking, until Jeanie came home. She walked past me as she always did, barely telling me hello. Before she was able to walk to the kitchen, I called out to her.

"Melvin tried to touch me."

She stopped and turned to me. "What you say, gyal?"

"Melvin was touching me." I answered.

"Where?" she asked.

I pointed to my chest and between my legs. Jeanie started laughing. A cruel laugh, where she leaned against the wall. She then stopped and stared at me.

"Oh, he touch your pum. Me na sure if you didn't like it or not. Me no believe you."

"Why don't you ask him?"

She smirked. "Why should I? Why he want a little ting

with no titties or ass? Me ya believe you if you wa Angie, and even den with her fast ass, I would tink she might try to fuck on him. Get out of here with di bullshit, gyal before you end up in a home."

I didn't say or eat nothing, or even move for the rest of the day. When Angie came home, I just stayed quiet, but Jeanie had to prove a point. As we laid on her couch, they were in her bed, making love. She had to put on a performance, making sure to let us know that she was the one Melvin wanted. However, that didn't change anything. It only made things worse. He knew he could get away with it and he did. I would lay still every night as he would creep out of my auntie's bedroom and would place his fingers and face on certain parts of my body. I had to keep myself from crying so I would allow myself to go to a faraway place. Back home, where my mom was still alive and my dad was still here. They took care of me and Angie. They loved us. It was a place where things never changed.

I really had nowhere to escape but in my own mind. There was no reprieve at school either. Ultimately, Angie and I were placed at another school in a year's time. Being the new girl in school, and with it being my eighth grade year and the last year of junior high, I didn't have time to really make any friends. I also began to sprout a little bit, hips and titties almost appearing overnight. I guess that came from Melvin. Needless to say, the boys liked it, but with all that and having long hair, the girls didn't. I was chased home, slammed into lockers and beaten up in the girl's bathrooms. Since Angie was at the high school, I didn't have her protection, so I had to fend for myself the best way I knew how. My sister and I went to a school that went from kindergarten up to 12th grade. Give or take a few new faces, we always moved up with the same group of people each year. No one knew me. All they knew was that I was new and that half the boys wanted to fuck me at school.

It took me two months before I finally had enough and struck out at these little bitches. I was walking out of the school when Jaya, an eighth grader who was in my math class, came up and pushed me from behind. I almost tripped but I was able to catch myself. I refused to turn around. I heard three other girls laugh with her. I kept it moving though. I just wanted to get home and try to get some homework done. She pushed me again.

"I knew this little bitch wasn't going to do anything. Other than try to fuck my man. Bitch if you ever..." Jaya began to yell.

And something in me snapped. Heavy with my math and science textbooks, I swung my backpack off of my arm and aimed for Jaya's face. There was a loud crack and a scream as my backpack connected with her face and broke her nose. Blood splattered everywhere. She grabbed her face and crumpled to the ground. Her three friends tried to pick her up. One of them looked as if they were going to charge towards me. I reached into my bag and pulled out my science book, ready to hit her if I had to. She put up her arms and backed away from me slowly. As I turned around to make my way home, she sneered at me.

"You are as good as dead."

I yelled back at her. "You can't do more to me than what's already been done."

"Whatever, bitch," she said. I didn't respond. I didn't care. I just wanted to get home.

I got home 20 minutes later. As usual, Angie wasn't there. I didn't really see her as much as I used to. I only saw her at night, right before I was about to go to bed. I didn't know what she was doing, but I couldn't blame her for not coming home. I would follow her lead if I also had somewhere else to go. But for now, the only place I had was Auntie Jeanie's and the safe place that I created in my mind. It was the only thing that kept me going. A couple hours later, I heard some banging and screaming at the door. I was getting used to hearing that since Melvin was the neighborhood dealer. Men and women screaming for a hit, willing to do anything to stay high. Melvin or Jeanie would come to the door and either give them their fix or shove them off the porch. They knew not to call on the cops on us. They were addicts, but they weren't stupid.

I ignored the knocks and screams on the outside of the door. Shortly after, I heard Jeanie stomping towards the door, cussing. I turned my head slightly as she opened up the door. I then returned to reading my book.

"What?" Jeanie screamed.

A familiar voice yelled, "Is that bitch Jahliyah here?"

My head snapped up at the sound of my name. "Fuck!"

My auntie turned towards me as a smirk crept across her face. "Jahliyah? You av visitors. Go on and take care of dis." She held the door open as I turned around and walked to the door. There were at least five girls out there, waiting to fuck me up. I was good as dead. They knew where I lived. At times, I was so eager to join my mama in Heaven, where I knew no harm would come to me. I was just too afraid to go through with it, even though the thought crossed my mind more than once. Maybe this was the moment I prayed for. I stepped out on faith outside of the house as Jeanie laughed and locked the door behind me.

I stood there and stared at the five girls. Neither of us made a move. One of them stepped towards me. I instinctively wrapped my hair up in a bun on the top of my head and took a fighting stance. Shaking her head, she stepped back and stood near Jaya who had a bandage on her nose.

"So, you're the shorty that hemmed up my sister?" she said to me.

I jutted out my chin and nodded my head.

"You Angie's sister, huh?" another one said.

I turned to her and nodded my head again. The other girls shook her head.

"I heard about what happened to your family." She then turned to Jaya and smacked her in the back of her head.

"You fuckin' with the wrong one. I'll tell you about it later. Let's go."

The girl pulled Jaya away and the other three girls

followed. I stood there, holding back the tears until they rounded the corner. I didn't want to go back inside the house, at least not yet. My aunt was willing to let me get my ass beat. I truly knew I had nowhere to go. The funny thing about the projects is that although it was a place of despair, they always had a playground. Oftentimes, it was used by the drug addicts, trapstars and pros, but it seemed as if it tried to provide a little bit of whimsy in an otherwise sad existence. Just a little glimmer of hope in a world full of hopelessness. It felt like that was the right place for me to be at the moment. I stepped off of the porch and turned the corner, walking towards the courtyard. For once, no one was there. I had the pocket park to myself. I walked over to the swing and threw my head back, looking at the sky as it started to turn pink and purple from the sunset. This was the first time I allowed myself to do this since my mother died. We used to watch the sunset together when she was alive.

I didn't know how long I was outside for, but I knew I had to be back to my aunt's house before it got too dark. I made it back just in time. I knocked on the door. After a few moments, the door slowly opened. It was Angie, her eyes red. She pulled the door open a little bit farther, allowing me to walk inside. I shut the door behind us as she walked over to the couch and sat down. The last few times I had seen Angie, her eyes were red as if she just finished crying. I didn't know what to say or do. As I sat down next to her, she curled up into a ball, resting her chin on her knees. She then turned to me and said,

"We are all we got. I'll get you out of this. Just hold on. I promise you, I will get you out of this."

I held back a sniffle as tears ran down my face. I leaned my head on my big sister's shoulder. She put her arm around me. It was time to go to sleep. It was Wednesday and we had school the next day.

That Wednesday was another day that I would never forget. It was the first day since the beginning of the school year where I didn't have to worry about being chased home. Jaya and her crew were extraordinarily nice to me that day. Not that they invited me to eat lunch with them, but they at least left me alone. The rest of the week, month and school year was pretty much the same. I stayed to myself, I didn't make any new friends that year, but at least I had some peace. It was refreshing not having to look over my shoulder. When the summertime hit, it was then that I found out that the reason why they left me alone was because they found out about what happened to my mother. A lot of the kids in the projects and at my school had lost their mothers in one way or another, through drug overdoses, incarceration or abandonment. They kind of saw me as one of their own, but I still talked and walked a little too funny for them. Despite our shared loss, me being a Capitol Hill girl was where they drew the line. The similarities for them stopped there.

The next three years of my life were pretty much the same and it became a blur. There wasn't much of a celebration for my eighth grade promotion. I wore Angie's hand-me-downs for my first day of ninth grade and continued to do so until I turned 16. I was lucky enough to have school be my escape where I was placed into the advancement placement classes. AP U.S. History fascinated me the most. Learning about how the capital of the U.S was moved from Philly to D.C. was amazing to me. It made me wonder how things may have been different if all of the nation's decisions were made on the other side of the Delaware River. I sympathized with the narratives of the slaves who came before me. I completely identified in wanting to escape a place where you were treated with such disgust but deep down knew there was no other way out.

All of that changed, however, when I turned sixteen, or should I say, when Angie turned eighteen. I remember it like it was yesterday. She came up to me and said,

"I didn't get you anything for your bday two months ago, because I had something better in mind. Now that I'm grown now, I got something to show you."

I looked up at her and smiled. As Angie grew older, she began to resemble our momma more and more. When I noticed this, it broke my heart and made it hard for me to look her in the face, especially since she took on the mama role when she shouldn't have had to. It got easier with time though. All we had was each other. Angie took my hand and led me out of our aunt's house. It was a hot DC summer day. I kept my hair curly because no matter how hard you trained your hair, that DC humidity could curl up the straightest Dominican blow out.

"Where are you taking me?" I asked.

She turned to me and smiled. "You'll see."

We walked past the park and down to the other side of the projects. We then stopped at apartment 116 as she reached into her pocket and took out a set of keys. She handed them to me.

"We got our freedom, Jahliyah," she said to me.

I looked down at the set of keys in my hand. I then reached over and placed them in the lock, opening the door. Inside was a dream. There was a new couch, flat screen TV, coffee table, a dining room table and chairs. I walked inside and went into the kitchen, where the refrigerator and cabinets were full of food and not roaches. I walked into the bedrooms and saw two full size beds with a nightstand, dresser and closet full of clothes. I ran back into the living room where Angie was sitting down on the couch.

"We're out tonight," she said to me.

"How did you afford all of these things?"

"Just workin'," she said. "Get the remainder of your stuff from Aunt Jeanie's house. Just go and if you see her, don't say anything to her. It's not like she'll miss us."

I nodded my head in excitement and ran out of the apartment. My heart was light, and filled with happiness. It took four years, but we finally had our freedom. I got back to Aunt Jeanie's quickly. Thank God, no one was home. I came inside and quickly put everything in my two duffel bags. I didn't even bother turning around to take one last look at that dump. I wasn't Lot's wife.

Nothing good ever came from looking back. I was back at my oasis, in my bedroom, away from all the bullshit. We finally had some peace and quiet. All we had was each other. I soon found out what she did for work. She became a stripper. It was the only thing that she could do with just a high school diploma that made some decent money. I felt so guilty and I didn't want the burden to be just on her. I had to do something. I had to make myself useful. So, I got a work permit from my school and got my first job at Footlocker in the mall.

And so it was like this for the last two years of high school for me. Angie was the only one clapping in the crowd for me when I received my diploma. Just like I was the only one at hers. We had to keep each other going. We imagined that our parents were there to see us, with my dad in the crowd somewhere and my mother cheering us on from Heaven. We would eventually go to college, but for the time being, we had to stack our bread and move to a better place. As long as we had each other though, we would be good.

CHAPTER 1

I hated taking the bus, but I would rather my sister have the car when she returned from the strip club. We'd had problems before where dudes tried to offer her rides home. I needed her to be safe and that was the best option for us as of now. I knew this path like the back of my hand, having walked it since my eleventh grade year of high school. It was three years later now and I was 19. I moved up over the three years that I'd been working at Footlocker. Now I was a manager. I really wanted to go to college, maybe major in business or something. Once I found the time to actually study, then I would make sure to go. I didn't want to waste my time. I put on my earbuds as I approached the bus stop. It was 9:30PM. I had to clear my mind so I would be able to go to sleep immediately once I got home. I had to open the next day.

I was at the bus stop for a few minutes when a man in a hoodie came up beside me. This was the other reason why I put my earbuds in. It protected me from having random dudes try to get at me. But tonight may have been the one time that was a mistake. He tried to get my attention, but I refused to answer him.

"Hey Miss? Can I ask you a question?" I heard him say over SZA. I refused to acknowledge him.

"Miss? Miss?" he asked again. I continued to stare straight ahead, waiting for the bus.

The next thing I knew, my head hit the side of the bus stop as he tried to pull my purse off of my shoulder. It dazed me but it was not enough to knock me out. I braced myself against the side of the bus stop and kicked him twice in the face. I then regained my footing, hitting him in the face with my elbow. He fell to the ground. I gave him one good kick and took off down the road. I ran as fast as I could, dodging and weaving to make sure that I wasn't being followed. Being raised in the projects definitely taught me what I needed to know to defend myself. I wanted to get home as soon as possible, so I ran to H Street and walked into the 7-11. I pulled out my phone and ordered a Lyft. Even though it was only five dollars or so to get home, I hated spending the money when I had a bus pass. I may need to take a new route home from now on. I wanted to avoid that happening again.

Instead of the usual hour to get home, it took all of ten minutes to get home. I missed having my own vehicle and would need to start saving up as soon as possible to make that a reality. I arrived at home and walked through the park to my apartment. I walked past Aunt Jeanie's house. To be honest I was completely unsure if she even still lived there. After we moved out, we hadn't so much as spoken to her or even called. She didn't return the favor either. I took out my keys and unlocked the door.

Home sweet home.

I dropped my stuff on the couch and walked straight to the bathroom. I knew that if I sat down for even a minute, I would've knocked out right there. I needed to wash the bullshit of the day off of me. Just as I was about to reach the bathroom, I heard a loud knock on the door. It was probably one of those busted ass niggas or some crackhead who was knocking around looking for a fix. Either way I didn't have time for it. I walked over to the shower. As I was about to turn it on, I heard my text message ping. No one texted me this time of the night so it had to be some kind of emergency. As if my night couldn't get any worse. I ran back into the living room and took my phone out of my purse.

It was a text from my best friend, Darryl. He was at the door.

I walked over to the door and there he was. He smiled at me as he walked inside. I closed the door as soon as he walked in. I gave Darryl a quick hug and I turned around to walk to my bedroom. He followed me. My boy had been home from college for a couple of weeks. He played basketball for FAMU, but he was also very smart, basically having a full ride academic scholarship. He was getting his college degree in business management. This was the same Darryl that everyone said I liked when I was twelve. He was the one who had seen me through everything, the only remnant I had of my old life. Even though he was miles away, doing big things, Darryl always still checked on me.

He sits on my bed as I sat at my desk chair.

"So we finally have a chance to chill, Ms. Busy. What you been up to?"

I smiled at him. "The same old, same old. Work, home, work, home. But enough about my shit. How are you?"

"Ball, business, bitches, the only BBB I'm concerned with."

I laughed. "I needed that after tonight."

His face looked concerned. "What happened? Them broke ass clowns outside still fucking with you?"

I shook my head. "No." I took a deep sigh. "I was almost robbed tonight while waiting at the bus stop. I was able to get away with all of my stuff, but I don't think I can take that route anymore. I don't want to be set up or anything."

I saw his jaw clench. It was something he always did when he was angry. "Where that nigga at though?" he said after a few moments of silence.

"There ain't much you can do about it now. Besides you got too much to lose. But I do want to thank you for wanting to take care of it for me."

"Always, Jae. Always." He responded, "Maybe I need to get some of this aggression off of me."

"What got you so riled up?"

"It's not so much being riled up. More like on some next level excitement shit."

Darryl stayed silent for a moment. I sat in my chair, fidgeting. He still didn't say anything. After what seemed like forever, I finally blurted out, "Well don't leave me hanging."

"Welp, you know how good we did last year in the finals."

"Yea," I said, nodding my head. "I watched you on TV."

"Well it's been confirmed that I will be starting in the upcoming season."

I leaned over and pushed him on the shoulder. "If you don't get on with your bad self. I am so proud of you." I then gave him a hug.

"Your opinion is the only one that matters, Jae. You just have to come out to see me play one day."

"If I can save up the money, you know I will," I replied.

I looked at the clock. It was 3 AM. I walked over to my bed and got under the covers. Like in the old days, Darryl laid next to me, on top of the covers. Before I knew it, it was morning.

Angie always worked overnight. She wasn't no dayshift bitch as she liked to call the strippers who worked in the afternoons. She kept her body fly so she worked the night when she was able to make the most money. Just as I was waking up, I saw her peak into my room and close the door behind her. I then went back to sleep. What fully woke me up was the sound of pans banging in the kitchen and a loud sigh. It may have been a rough night for her as well. I sat up in bed which caused Darryl to turn around and open his eyes. He sat up slowly and looked at his watch.

"Shit. It's about that time," he said, groggily. I smiled at him. He stood up and picked up his bag.

"You sure you good, ma?"

"I've been through worse than this," I said as we exited my bedroom. Darryl was the only boy that Angie allowed to spend the night. She didn't want people knowing exactly where we lived. In fact, we still lived in the same complex as my aunt and even she still didn't know what apartment we stayed in. Every dude was like Melvin to my sister and I. Best to keep them away as much as possible. But Darryl, that was like her little brother. He would always have a place to stay if he needed us.

We walked down the short hallway and pass the kitchen. Angie was at the stove, cooking up some eggs and French toast. The vanilla smell was intoxicating.

Just as we reached the front door, Angie looked up and smiled.

"Hey Darryl."

"Hey Angie."

She winked at him. "I'm so proud of you. Continue to represent DC for us."

He smiled at her. He always had a slight crush on her. Angie stayed trying to link us up but it was her that he was feeling. Ten years and there was no letting up. He felt he would save her one day. I hoped he would. He stared at her as she turned back around to finish our plates. Moments later, she turned around with a plate in her hand. She walked up to Darryl and handed him a plate.

"Here," she said, "Something for the road."

"Thank you," he stuttered as his eyes became dreamy. I shook my head and pushed him out the door. We gave each other a hug and I pushed him out the door.

"Let me know you're in safe."

"Don't I always?"

I shut the door behind me. I sat down at the kitchen

table as Angie finished setting out the plates. French toasts and over-medium eggs were my favorite. I immediately dug in.

"Darryl doesn't normally spend the night. Is there something you want to tell me?"

I shook my head.

Angie took a bite of her food and smirked. "Girl, stop lying. You don't lay in bed with a man and nothing happens."

I shook my head again. "Nope, nothing on that front. However, I was almost robbed yesterday."

I saw Angie's smile disappear. "What?"

I shrugged my shoulders and continued. "It was bound to happen. It's the hood. I was waiting at the bus stop when this guy asked me a question. Next thing he did was try to reach over and take my bag. I got away though. I'm fine. Really."

Angie's eyes narrowed, one of her telltale signs that she was pissed. "That's it. You're taking the car."

I shook my head no. What she did was even more dangerous than me taking the bus home after work. She had niggas who may not take no for answer and then she would be gone. She was all I had. I couldn't take losing her also. I didn't know what I would do.

"Before you say anything Jae, remember, I leave when the day breaks. I'll be fine. I can get a ride with one of the homegirls until I get another car," Angie said to me soothingly. "I can't risk losing you. You're all I have."

I looked up at her and smiled. We both had the same fears about each other. I nodded my head in surrender. "Fine. As long as I know you're safe."

"Good." Angie replied. She looked at her watch and then walked over to her purse. "The keys are on the table. I'll be right back."

I loved Angie with all my heart, but there were some things I got mad with her about. I knew where she was going. I knew who the money was for. And it just wasn't right. That woman did nothing for us. I acted like I didn't know because I didn't want to argue with the only person I truly had left in this world. I was reluctant now to take the car because I didn't want her to use that against me, to have me give money to Jeanie and her dude. I took the long way through the apartments so I avoided walking past their house. I didn't even know that they still lived here until I peeped game on what Angie was doing.

I didn't want to dwell on it. Too much had happened already. I waited however to make sure that she came back home safely. I was just finishing up my meal as she walked back into the house. She just gave me a look and kind of smiled. I just stared at her before going back to my room. I had to resign myself to thinking that it was her money so she could do as she pleased. I couldn't stop her any other way.

CHAPTER 2

The day went by fast. I drove the car home. It was amazing how much time you saved when you drove home. What was normally an hour long bus ride was only a 15 minute drive home. I could definitely get used to this, especially on the days where I was exhausted. I managed to stay upbeat for most of the day. Serving as a manager at Foot Locker meant I had to make sure that everything was closed out properly before closing. Luckily, today was a slow day so I finished on time. I parked in our space and made my way to our apartment. As soon I entered the house however, I became overwhelmed with sleepiness. I felt as if I couldn't even make it to my bedroom which was only fifteen feet away down the hallway. I sat on the couch, utterly exhausted. I laid down, not even bothering to wrap my hair up. The next thing I knew, it was the morning.

Even though you can be in the same surroundings for a lot of your life, sometimes waking up in a different part of the room can change your perspective on everything. The windows in my bedroom faced the outside of the apartment, where I could see the hustle and bustle of city life. Even though it was the poor, they were still going about their business. Going to work or school every day, just trying to make their future better than their past. However, when looking out the living room window, I saw the interior of the projects.

As my eyes focused, I noticed how the sun didn't shine as bright in our complex. I saw the trapstars outside making their deals. The hoes coming back from the night shift. It was depressing. I wanted, no, NEEDED more out of life than what I currently had, but I honestly didn't know how to get more. The hood did that to you. You knew more was out there but it made you feel trapped. I would eventually figure it out before this took me under. I'd been here most of my young life. I couldn't live the next fifty years like this. I refused.

I finally got up and walked over to the bathroom. I

turned on the shower and wrapped up my hair. I stepped into the shower and reached for my passionfruit shower cream. It was luxurious. It was expensive. And it smelled amazing. It was one of the few luxuries I allowed myself. I heard the door open and shut. Angie was home. I closed my eyes and let the warm water soothe me. A thought crossed my mind as I opened my eyes and looked at my body. My body had shaped out pretty nicely. I mean I didn't have the fat ass and titties that Angie had, but I had some curves to me and a flat stomach. I could probably do nice as a stripper. Both of us bringing in that kind of dough would mean we would be out of here in no time. But I knew I could never do it. I was a wreck in interviews so I knew I could never take my clothes off and dance in front of people. I was way too shy.

I got out of the shower and headed towards my bedroom. Angie was on her bed, on top of her covers, knocked out. It must have been a long night for her. I went into my bedroom and got dressed in the familiar striped shirt and black pants. I put some conditioner in my hair. After applying some lip gloss, I left my room and headed towards the kitchen. I pulled out the left-overs and stuffed them in my bag. I picked up the car keys and slowly closed the door behind me, being careful not to wake Angie up. The drive to work was equally as quick. I got there about thirty minutes before my start time. I smiled as I leaned back in the car. I finally had some me time where I could just relax before I started my day dealing with crazy ass customers. The public could be real petty sometimes. It took a special type of person to work in retail.

And today proved to be one of those days.

From the minute I stepped in at work, it was nothing but bullshit. I never understood why people got off on treating those that work in retail with so much disdain. The over the top attitudes from these basic bitches was too much for me. I learned to control my temper but some things shouldn't be condoned. And if the attitudes from these DD's discounts ass bitches wasn't enough, our systems were down and all we could do was accept cash. No one carries cash anymore. So, when lunchtime rolled around, I knew I needed to calm myself down before I made a terrible mistake. I brought my lunch but I just couldn't stand the thought of even being in the building. So I decided to eat my lunch outside. It was early October which meant the weather was still good. It was be a month or so before we started seeing the first snow. I had to enjoy it as much as I could.

I worked near the Eight Twenty Five building in DC,

which is one of the most luxurious mixed use spaces in Washington. The place had everything a girl could dream of: Rag and Bone, Louis Vuitton, Kate Spade and Gucci. All the places I wish I could shop at but couldn't afford. For someone without a good job and an education I didn't want to do the things necessary to be able to afford it. I sat down at one of the outside tables and took a few deep breaths before unpacking my lunch. I was about to take out my cell phone when I heard a familiar voice call my name.

"Jae? Jae, is that you?" I looked up and saw Shayla, one of the few friends I made from high school. I was really close to Shayla in high school. She was a pretty girl who stood at 5'7" with black hair. Back in the day, she used to wear her hair in cornrows but now she upgraded to those beautiful Ethiopian Goddess braids, a homage to her mom's heritage. Her light skin, the same color as creamy coffee reflected her dad's Puerto Rican background. She was on the thicker side, but like Angie she always wore her curves well and caused all of the boys to do her bidding and some of mine as well. We hadn't seen each other since high school, which was about a year ago. She ran up to me, excited. I took a deep sigh as I stood up and gave her a big hug.

"Girl, it has been forever. How have you been?" Shayla continued.

I smiled. "It's been going." We sat back down. It was then that I was able to get a good look at her. This girl had definitely bossed her life up. She was designered out. Her hair was flawless and her face was beat to the Gods. I also noticed that she had a shit ton of high end shopping bags. Shayla didn't go to college so I didn't know where she got her dough from, but at the same time, I hadn't seen her in DC in a long while. I felt a little pang of envy but I had to disguise it on my face. I already felt bad enough.

"How have you been?" I asked her.

She winked at me. "My life has been great ever since I got hooked up with the game."

"The game?" I asked, "You mean, stripping? Naw I'm good on all that."

"Tuh, girl please. Any bitch can strip now. It's not even an art anymore. I'm on a more elevated level. I'm a sugar baby and I got a sugar daddy who cashes me out. Look, I'm too pretty to be working at the mall like these broke hoes." She then paused and looked at my FootLocker uniform. She swallowed hard but continued, "Present company excluded, but why work, when I can get me an older white man that can cash me out?"

I thought about the idea. Even though I really liked the sound of having a man take care of me, I just couldn't help but think it was something like prostitution. I've never really been with anyone in that way, so, I wasn't sure if I wanted to give it up to someone that I didn't really care about.

"What exactly is a sugar baby?" I asked.

"It's a younger woman who is paid to be in the company of an older, wealthier man. He takes you shopping and on expensive trips. And before you ask, it's not prostitution. It's companionship. If you decide to let him smash, that is on you. Sometimes, it's fun though."

I took a sip of my drink. She continued,

"You way too cute for all this bullshit you going through. Ratchet ass customers, low pay. Come on mamas, you better than that. I can put you on if you want to see what it's like."

All I could do was nod my head. "I'll think about it. My number is the still the same as in high school. Hit me up."

She winked at me. "Will do."

I looked back at my watch. My lunch break was over. Time to return to hell.

The rest of the day was a little bit better. I once again pulled a damn near twelve hour shift. I just didn't understand at times where the money went. But I knew I didn't have any in my pockets. That really needed to change. I drove home after closing up shop, with my mind wandering to the conversation I had with Shayla earlier that afternoon. I never dated white men before; I never really been interested in them. But at the same time, niggas weren't paying like they weigh and as I thought about it, a little money for giving someone her time couldn't hurt. As long as I wasn't fucking, it would be all good. I got out of the car and made my way to the apartment. As I approached the door, I saw a familiar, male figure waiting near the doorway. It was Darryl, making sure I was safe. I smiled as I unlocked the door. We quickly made our way inside.

He followed me to my bedroom where I put down my bag and sat on my bed. My shoulders sagged before I collapsed on the bed.

"One of those days, huh?" Darryl said as he sat at my desk.

"As always. Guess who I saw?"

"Who?" he asked.

"Remember Shayla Rodriguez?"

He paused for a second. "The Ethiopian chick with the fat ass?"

"If that's the only thing you remember about her, then yes, her," I retorted. "I ran into her today. We had a chance to catch up during my lunch break."

"How is she doing?"

"Her life is lit as fuck. I ain't even mad at her. Good to see some of the females I knew doing good out here."

Darryl nodded his head. "Well, I got word today about me and playing ball."

I sat up and smiled. "I got the chance to watch you start. You were amazing out there."

"Thank you. You're not the only one who noticed. I spoke to my coach and he said some scouts have been asking about me. All in all, if I stand out this season, I will definitely be drafted by a pro team. Then we'll be good, family. I always told you I got you."

I walked over and gave my best friend a hug. I was so

proud of him, but I didn't want to wait until Darryl was drafted for things to be good. I'd had to take care of myself since I was twelve. I had to figure things out. Just as I was about to lay back down, I heard a loud, hard knock at the door. Darryl got up to answer as he always did in case the situation became dangerous. I walked behind him, grabbing the knife that I kept at my bedside in case he needed backup. He walked over and opened the door. Standing outside were two police officers.

"Can I help you?" Darryl asked.

"Sir, is there a Melvin Thomas that lives here?"

I stood next to Darryl at the entrance of the door. "Melvin doesn't live here," I answered.

"Do you know where he is, ma'am?"

I looked at Darryl quickly then back at the officer. I shook my head. "I don't know where he is, but he is not here."

"Then you won't mind if we take a quick look around," the police officer said as they pushed their way into the house. I didn't even want to argue with them so I just watched as they looked around and knocked a few things over. All this passive aggressive grandstanding as they "looked" for Melvin. The place was small so I knew they wouldn't be here for too much longer. Darryl and I stood near the door with our hands in plain sight. We didn't want to give them any reason to take another young black life. After a few more moments of messing up my house, they walked back to the door. Before leaving, he turned to me.

"Please call us if you see him." He handed me a card.

I nodded my head. "We will, officer. Thank you." I said as I took the card from him and slid it into my pocket. We closed the door behind them and sat on the couch.

"I'm not leaving until shit blows over."

"Thanks," I said as I turned on the TV.

A few hours must have passed by when we heard another knock at the door. Darryl stood up and walked over.

"I hope it ain't the police again." He said as he opened the door. He was taken aback. It was Melvin. I stood up as he eyed me. Darryl noticed and stepped between us.

"What are you doing here?" Darryl said to him.

"I heard the police were over here a few hours ago. Did you say anything to them?"

"We should have," Darryl said, smiling. I watched as Melvin grabbed his chin and nodded his head. He then pushed Darryl back. I stood up and grabbed the knife that we kept near the end table as Darryl stumbled backwards. Darryl then lunged himself forward to push Melvin back when Melvin pulled a gun on him. My heart stopped as Darryl stopped and put his hands up in the air. I couldn't let the only good guy I knew end up dead. I had to think fast. I did the only thing I could do which was stand in front of Darryl. I knew Melvin still would try it with me, so I hoped that it would make him stop.

"Please, you don't want to do this. They are already looking for you. They might still be in the complex. No one said anything. You know I don't snitch. Just please go and hide somewhere," I pleaded.

I felt Darryl move away from me. Melvin's eyes were fixated on me. I had him where I wanted him. Darryl all of a sudden rushed towards him, punching him, which caused him to drop the gun. Melvin stumbled backwards as Darryl picked up the gun from the floor. He then pointed it at him. It was so heartbreaking to watch. I never thought I would see my best friend ever be in this situation. It was indeed hard for a brother in this world. When Melvin regained his composure, he looked at Darryl and laughed.

"You ain't gonna pull no trigger. Go back to reading books, school nigga."

Darryl kept the gun pointed at Melvin as he walked over to the side of the building and reached down. I looked over and saw that he had Aunt Jeanie, all strung out. He then threw her on our living room floor.

"She's not my problem anymore." Melvin then put his hands up in the air, smiling and walked away from our door. Darryl didn't lower the gun until I closed the door. I looked down at my crackhead aunt on the floor. I stayed away from her for three years and now here she was at my doorstep. I couldn't do this. Enough was enough. Leaving her on the floor, I went back into my bedroom and picked up my cell phone. I found Shayla's number and texted her these two words.

"I'm in."

CHAPTER 3

Shayla agreed to meet with me at my lunch break the next day. From that early morning as I packed my bag for work, I thought about how far I would go to get what I needed. I would take my lunch at around 3:30 PM. This would give me plenty of time to actually enjoy my lunch and listen. That time was usually the slowest time of the day. Everything would pick up around five or so, when people were getting off of work. The day went by pretty quickly and relatively smooth. Not too many bullshit customers that made me want to pull my hair out. It was getting close to the holiday season so I made sure to appreciate these easier days. Then I thought about it; if I enjoyed the sugar baby life, I might not be working here during that time. I walked out the house and locked the door when I heard a familiar voice call out to me. It was Darryl.

"I should've thought of walking you home earlier, but now that you're using the car to get home, I can keep you company before I go back to school. Maybe I can meet up with you for lunch?"

I shifted my bag to my left shoulder as we both walked to the car. "I don't want to turn you down, but I already have plans for lunch."

"Who do you have plans with? Maybe I can join you."

I didn't want to tell him anything. I wanted to keep what I was doing a secret. So I lied to him for the first time in our ten years of friendship. "It's a working lunch. Team meeting with a district manager. I wish you could go but..."

Darryl nodded his head. "I understand. Make your shmoney. I'll hang out with you tonight."

I smiled at him. "Alright, bet."

The time went by quickly. Next thing I knew it was 3:30 PM. I went into the break room and took out my lunch bag. I walked the few blocks over to Eight Twenty Five. Shayla was already there when I arrived. She looked me up and down and smiled.

"Lunch was on me. Save that for the next day," she said

as I sat down across from her. I shrugged my shoulders and picked up a menu.

"So you decided to come to the dark side. It's not as bad as you think. The only bitches that talk shit about what we do are either ugly bitches or broke hoes. If you got beauty and personality, there is never a reason why you shouldn't be living lavish."

I just nodded my head. Shayla continued,

"I promise you, Jae. If you work hard, you can move out of the projects and your sister can even stop stripping."

My eyes widened as I really thought about it. Angie had made so many concessions for me. Stripping so that she could take care of us. I knew that was never what she wanted to do but she was backed into a corner, acting as a mother figure and doing what she could to take care of us. We needed money fast, and for a female with no real skills, stripping was the only way to get that. I wanted to make her life easier.

"Getting into the game is easy. There's several websites that you can post on. The one that seemed to work the best for me was sugarbabesforyou.com."

I took out my phone and typed the name down on my notepad.

"I can guarantee you that you would get hits within the hour. You then look over the profiles and choose which one or ones are best for you," she said, making quotation mark gestures with her hands.

"Make sure to put an okay photo of yourself on your profile. You want to surprise these men when you see them."

I continued to take notes on my phone.

Shayla continued, "Let me make some comparisons for you, between the strippers and the sugar babies. This is something that needs to be put to rest so you really understand. While I respect the hustle, strippers are subjected to hoping that whatever man who comes into the strip club makes it rain on them, but as a sugar baby, you get to choose who you deal with and the rewards are guaranteed."

I nodded my head in agreement. Even though Angie was bad as fuck, there were some nights where her take wasn't as high as it normally would be, and the month would be lean. I definitely wanted to be put on.

"However, if you do want to be more discreet, in case you want a future in the public eye, I will give you this card."

Shayla reached into her Birkin and pulled out a business card. I looked at the card and then back up at Shayla.

"I'll be at work at that time."

"Come over after work. The door is always open. I'll see you later."

Before she stood up, she reached into her wallet and pulled out a one hundred dollar bill.

"Get whatever you want. See you soon." And then she was gone. I looked back down at the card. A million thoughts flooded my head. I didn't know what to do, or if this was something that I should even be doing. But then I thought about Melvin, my aunt, and how Angie had been stripping for years. I owed this to us, so that we could finally have some peace. I would go.

I got home around the normal time. As I approached my doorstep, Darryl was there, waiting for me.

"How did the lunch meeting go? It would be okay if it was an actual date, you could've told me," he said as I opened the door. I laughed as we entered the house.

"No," I said just as the unmistakable pop of gunshots rang out. We both instinctively hit the floor. Darryl kicked the door shut and locked it before laying down on his back. We just laid on the floor as we heard yelling. Growing up in the hood, you stayed low and waited until everything died down.

Darryl turned to face me. "I can't wait to get out of here. I'm tired of my strung out ass mom. We lost everything and had to come here. We all have to come here when shit fucks up. I'm tired of always worrying about getting shot and other shit like this. This can't be life. I hate leaving you here, but I have to go to make things better for us.

A single tear slid down my face. It's crazy what we go through. What we are willing to do to get away from our conditions can sometimes surprise us. I reached over and grabbed his hand. I squeezed as tight as I could.

"You're not the only one who can make things better. I have a plan to get us out of this."

CHAPTER 4

So it was after work, and here I was standing in front of this nice, large building. I took a deep breath as I walked inside to the office. I gave my name to the receptionist.

"Jahliyah Robinson. We were expecting you." I was taken aback. I hadn't made a call or anything. Before I could ask any more questions, another woman appeared and I was escorted to the elevator. Once we stepped inside the elevator, she took out a key card and pressed the button for the tenth floor. We zoomed up to the tenth floor and the doors opened. We walked into a gorgeous all-white lobby. However, I wasn't able to take in my surroundings because I was immediately led to an immaculate office, where this gorgeous, dark-haired white woman was standing looking at the view from her window. It was a view of the Washington Monument.

She turned around and sized me up. She then smiled.

"You know the Washington Monument is just a large phallic symbol. Showing the power of the United States and its standing in the world. The problem is, the real power is within the Yoni, or the pussy. From this, we women can give pleasure, profit or pain."

I stood there at the door, listening to every word she said. Everything in here was expensive. Erica was dressed to perfection, down to the Red bottom nude Pigalles that adorned her feet. I didn't even know how to answer. I was honestly afraid to sit down. Everything was gorgeous and blistering white and here I was in my FootLocker work uniform. I didn't belong. I felt dirty. The woman walked back to her desk and sat down.

"Please. Sit," she continued. I walked over to the desk and sat in the chair in front of her.

"Shayla's had great things to say about her but she didn't do you justice. You are absolutely stunning and I'm happy that you decided to hear more about what we do."

"Shayla already explained some things to me, but I

would like to hear more. If there is anything else I need to know," I said.

Erica nodded her head slightly and placed her perfectly manicured hands underneath her chin. "Well, tell me why you are here. That way I can tailor the information to help you."

I took a deep sigh. "I hope that I can find a sugar daddy. I don't want bags or to travel. I just want to at least get me and my sister out of the projects. Somewhere safe, somewhere where we can actually thrive despite what we've been through."

Erica nodded her head sympathetically. She put her hands down on the table. "I understand your frustration because I may not look like it but I came from the projects, just like you. My real name is Erica Arroyo but Cline has a nicer ring to it, if you get what I'm saying. However, despite all of that, I transcended into something great and I wanted to share it with other young women. We already don't get paid the same amount as men, so we might as well get our just due in another way."

I nodded my head in agreement. She continued,

"The sugar baby is a woman who is cultured, classy and

beautiful. She is well put-together and offers the distinguished gentleman much needed companionship and comfort. Don't let the media tell you otherwise. There is big business in governing and policing how women use their bodies. You'd be perfect because you're pretty and young. I am going to be honest with you. You seem a little rough around the edges, but the projects will do that to you. I will put you through some etiquette trainings and you'll receive a makeover. All of this we will pay for because our clients prefer the company of classy women."

I continued to nod my head, trying to absorb everything that was being told to me.

"You do understand that you will have to quit your job so you'll have time to attend all of the trainings."

That made me stop in my tracks. I couldn't have my sister do all the work, plus eventually she would find out and I wouldn't know how I could explain this to her. I had to make this commitment. I was going to do this. Erica reached into her desk and pulled out a few pieces of paper on a gold-trimmed clipboard. She handed me a Mont Blanc pen.

"These contracts basically say that the fees are paid by the client and that there is a six-month commitment with an option to renew after the end of the contract period. If you leave any earlier, you must pay back a prorated amount for each of the trainings, classes and anything else we provide you."

I nodded my head again and signed the three pages. She smiled as I handed back the pen and the clipboard.

"Be back at the office tomorrow morning, ten AM.

Everything was a blur, and the next thing I knew I was back outside, standing in front of the car. I took out my cell phone and dialed my district manager. I told him that I had a family emergency where I would have to use all of my sick time and the little bit of vacation saved up to take care of it. It technically wasn't a lie. I was lucky that I was cool with my DM. He was okay with everything. I hung up and took a deep breath. I then got out of the car and drove home. I walked into my house and saw my aunt strung out, laying up on the couch. She hadn't moved the whole day. I walked straight into the bedroom and changed into my pajamas. I just sat down on my bed and looked at my surroundings. We are going to get out of this situation, come hell or high water.

I woke up in the morning and headed straight to the office. The classes were all held in the office. Some of the most beautiful women I'd ever seen taught us everything that we needed to know on how to be the proper companion to our clients. Etiquette and charm school classes included holding conversations about current events, the arts, and politics. All of this was necessary in how I would handle myself in certain high society situations such as the opera, a political event, dinners and other activities. I learned that this particular company catered to wealthy white men who wanted women for companionship. Some of their clientele was married, some were single, but what they had in common was that they all had a penchant for women of color.

During one of my classes, I had to ask the question, so I raised my hand,

"Do we have to have sex with the men that we are partnered with?"

Erica turned to me and smiled. "That's all your choices to do so. Go with what you feel is right."

I sat back, not completely satisfied with the answer. Something about the way Erica responded made me feel like she wasn't being honest with us.

Erica continued, "We're not like escorts where men hire us for a night or a weekend. Being a sugar baby is a lifestyle."

I actually did better than I thought I would. Even though I finished all of my workshops, I still couldn't shake the feeling that Erica wasn't giving me the whole story. I vowed to myself that I would make it my choice regardless of what the man may want from me. It was the end of the week, and I already had my first date. I was going to a gala with an older gentleman and I needed to spruce myself up. Most of my dresses came from Macy's and although they were cute, they weren't quite gala ready. So basically, Erica told me that it was my time to get my makeover. Erica took me shopping at all the places that I only dreamed of. Louis Vuitton, Gucci, Chanel, 3.1 Phillip Lim and Acne Studios. Gorgeous dresses that I had only seen on actresses and the models in the magazines. She got my hair blown out and took me to a makeup artist. When I was finally done by 7:30, I took a final look at myself and couldn't believe what I saw looking back at me. I literally transformed into a more natural looking Instagram model. It was then I realized, that no one was really ugly, they just needed the right guidance to be their best self. I looked gorgeous and I felt ready for my first date.

So as I waited in the lobby, Erica sat across from me and gave me the rundown.

"Your first client's name is Blake Austin. He's a multi-millionaire who is married, but is looking for a sugar baby to accompany him across the country for several trips, while his wife is vacationing for a month in the Maldives. Blake is one of our best clients and is really a great guy. He is mostly attracted to Black women, but he married his wife for appearances."

"What type of appearances?" I said, indignantly.

Erica pursed her lips. "It was a different time back then. He has been married for over fifteen years. The upper echelon has a different mindset than the others do."

She narrowed her eyes at me to see if I understood. I did, very well. It rubbed me the wrong way, but I had to do this.

"Your limo will be here soon. It will take you to his address and then it's on. Good luck."

I smiled and nodded.

CHAPTER 5

When the limo stopped at his penthouse, my heart sank. I never saw a picture of him so I didn't know what to expect. It wasn't that white men weren't my thing, it's just that I never really saw myself with one, especially an older one. It was something that my dad used to tell me, that he would never see me as an equal, that I would be something exotic to him. That's why Erica's comment about marrying his wife for appearances really bothered me. I never understood what was so bad about us as a people. We had our problems, but all people did. I tried to stay the intense beating of my heart as I waited for Blake to get into the limo. Shortly after, the driver got out of the car and opened up the door. And there he was.

He was absolutely gorgeous. Blake was 6'1, with clear,

tanned skinned. His hair was short and wavy, dark with touches of gray here and there. But it was his eyes that struck me. They were this amazing, piercing blue that sucked you in. He looked a lot younger than I thought he would. He seemed like he was in his late 30's, so Erica's comment was starting to really have me feeling some type of way. He was also built with his suit cut to perfection. I could smell the wealth on him.

Oh my.

He also seemed taken aback. As he situated himself in the car, he stared back at me. The driver closed the door behind him. The car started moving forward. We sat in silence. I didn't want to get a bad review, so I decided I would be the first to speak.

"Mr. Austin??"

"Please, Jahliyah," he said in a smooth, deep voice. "Please call me Blake."

"Blake?"

"My God, you are gorgeous."

I was taken aback. I never heard anyone say that about me before. I smiled.

"Kind of shy too. I like that."

I stayed quiet. I didn't know what to say.

"We will be going to the DC Gala tonight. This is where all of the politicos in Washington, meet and party. Then after that, who knows..." he continued with a wink.

The limo arrived at the Sofitel, right across from the Capitol Building. Where my mom used to work. My heart dropped at the memory of my mother—that was until he grabbed my hand, and tickled the inside of my palm with his middle finger. It soothed me.

"Ready for your debut?"

I smiled at him and nodded. "Born ready."

I DIDN'T SLEEP with him the first time, nor the second or third, even though I wanted to. Nor did he pressure me. I could tell he wanted to, but I was used to that with the few guys I dated. I knew how to navigate them. I had never really been out with a white man before, especially an older one. In the DC circles, he was well-known and no one seemed to bat an eye when we were together. He showed me a life that I only saw on TV. Shopping, fine dining, and dinners on yachts. I was usually the only one of my kind at these events. Not even the wait staff was black or brown. It was sad that most people who looked like me would never get a chance to experience this.

Blake would pay me after every night on top of the gifts and dates. Three thousand dollars each time. I had to be careful how I worked it. I put half of the money in the bank and the other half I hid at home. Bitches chased bags all the time and I didn't want to be the one chick that the banks tried to expose. When I would go home, I did my best to avoid my sister. I knew for a fact she would notice these changes and I didn't have the time or even the mental capacity to lie to her. Thank God it wasn't hard to do, because Angie worked late hours and was usually asleep when I got home and when it was time for me to leave. The days were magical but I couldn't tell Darryl about anything I did. But I was sure he would say something soon enough. As much as I tried to hide it, the neighbors were starting to see the changes in me, how I looked different and how I was getting picked up and dropped off from a limo every night.

I overheard the rumors. Hating ass bitches selling their pussy for chicken nuggets and a blunt commenting on me, saying shit like she's prostituting, or she stripping, or dating a drug dealer because my come up was solid.

What the bitches didn't understand was that I was still in the hood with them, so I wasn't doing that well. While all this talk was going on, I just stayed stacking. As I came home one day from grocery shopping, there was Darryl, waiting at my door step. I knew this day would come. He walked over and took the two bags from me. I opened up the door and we walked inside. He walked into the kitchen and sat the bags down on the counter. I stood near the sink waiting for him to ask. He didn't hesitate.

"So are the rumors true?"

I gave him the side eye. "How long have I avoided that life, to start now? You think I want to end up like any of these ratchets we live next to? Or even possibly end up like my auntie?"

He shook his head no.

"Remember when we were young and niggas would talk shit. People never seem to grow up from high school. Hell, middle school for some."

He nodded his head again and smiled. He gave me a once over. "So then why you lookin' fancy? Like you flexin' for the gram?"

I took a deep sigh. I hated lying to him. "I'm getting

older so I decided to update my look. I really don't have money like that. It's amazing what you can find at some of these rich lady thrift stores. I think they call them consignment.

"Look, I believe you Jae. It's just that I want you to be careful. People don't like to see other people doing good and I don't want you to get robbed or hurt. I don't know what I would do, and I got a lot to lose."

"I know, but it's all a part of the master plan. Just trust me."

"Alright, bet."

I looked at my watch. "I gotta freshen up for work. I'll call you later."

"Okay. Later."

I waited until he left the house before I locked the door behind him and got in the shower. It was almost five o'clock and I had an early evening date with Blake. I was wondering where he was going to take me this time. I got dressed quickly and waited for my limo to arrive. When I received the call that the driver was here, I picked up my purse and walked outside. Just as I was about to lock the door, I was grabbed from behind and thrown against the wall near the corner of my building. It was Melvin.

He put his hand around my neck and with his face close to mine, he said,

"If you wanted to have sex for money, all you had to do was ask." His breath was tart. It suffocated me. I tried to fight him off, but I couldn't. I was starting to get light headed as he squeezed my throat and dragged me into a dark corner of the projects building. He started groping me, trying to slide his hand into my panties, when all of a sudden, I heard a sizzling sound. Melvin shook and then fell to the ground. I recognized Shayla as she continued to taser him. I wondered briefly why Shayla was here, but I didn't care. She saved me. I was still intact.

"Come on. Let's go," she said as she extended her hand. I took it and we ran to the limo. We got in the car and we drove off.

"You're going to need this," she said as she handed me the taser. "This will be your new best friend."

I nodded my head and put the tiny taser into my purse. She smoothed my hair.

"I know you're wondering why I'm here. It ain't that type of party."

I nodded my head.

"I just wanted to know how it's going with Blake. If there was anything you wanted to discuss. You got one of the best ones. I just wanted to make sure that everything was okay because certain things can happen. I never really gave you some of the dos and don'ts of being a sugar baby. Main do is always be discreet, the main don't is falling in love with any sugar daddy. You're supposed to be in love with the lifestyle, not the man. You promise me that?"

"I promise. You already know why I'm doing this," I said.

Shayla winked at me. "I know."

After dropping Shayla off, the limo stopped in front of the Hamilton Hotel. I'd only read about this place. I never thought I would ever set foot in here, not even as an employee. And yet, here I was. I was anticipating what would happen next. I received a text on my phone.

"Meet me at the bar."

I walked inside and to the left.

And there he was.

Blake stood up as I walked to him. I was always shocked by how handsome he was. He was wearing a tan sports coat with fitted dark rinse jeans, a white button down and tan Louis Vuitton boat shoes. I was wearing a bright red Oscar De La Renta mini dress with Roger Vivier heels. My hair was curled to one side and cardinal red lipstick finished the look. Blake gave me the once over.

"Stunning as always."

"Likewise," I said as he took my hand and kissed it. We sat down at one of his private tables.

"Each day I see you is like a new lease on life. Everything is more potent, more intense. You truly are something amazing, Miss Jahliyah."

I blushed. He always had something to say that left me speechless. I didn't know how to match his words. All I could do was just nod my head and smile. He knew I wasn't mute. I would have to let him know how I was one way or another. Tonight might be the night. The waiter handed us the menus.

"The wings and the lobster bisque are the best in the city. They also have boozy milkshakes here too. The place is laid back. I don't always want you around just for galas; we can just hang out and shoot the shit. That might help you open up a little bit more," he said gently.

I nodded. "Thank you," I said. "I just don't want to say the wrong thing."

"Why would you think that?" he asked.

"It's DC. Anything can be the wrong thing."

He laughed. "That is true."

The waiter came back and took our order. Blake ordered two plates of wings, two lobster bisques, a gin and tonic for himself and a boozy bananas foster shake for me. I wasn't quite twenty one yet, but a little liquor never really hurt anyone.

"I don't want this to come off the wrong way, but I wonder, what do you do for work? I mean we have been to many political events and I've never seen your face in the papers as a representative or anything."

He raised his left eyebrow at me and my heart sank. I thought I fucked up. We were silent until the waiter came back with our drinks. I nervously sipped my shake. I fucked up and Erica was going to hear about it.

"I just wanted to know because my parents used to work in government. At the capitol building to be exact. I..."

"No need to be nervous; you didn't do anything wrong. Actually, you're the first one to ask me that."

I took a deep sigh of relief. He saw my nervousness melt away. He smiled and continued,

"I am a political consultant for the Democratic Party. A strategist would best describe me."

"That's amazing. Is it really like House of Cards?"

He laughed and shook his head. "House of Cards doesn't have shit on the real DC. The stories I may tell you one day. That is, if you want to continue this."

"I do."

The food came shortly after. Blake wasn't lying. The wings and the sauce were good. The lobster bisque was also on point. It was so much more relaxed than all the other events that we had gone to over the last few weeks. He was a really sweet and kind man. A true gentleman. I wasn't used to anyone like this where I came from— well aside from Darryl. Most dudes were full of shit and didn't even try to fake it to get at the panties. Where you stopped, there would be another female who would gladly continue. Needless to say that's why I kept my v-card intact. We spent the whole time at the Hamilton, just laughing and talking. I let him talk about himself more; where he went to school and his business. He was truly privileged, a life that was completely different from mine. After a few hours, he looked at his watch and smiled at me. I smiled back.

It was time to call it a night. Blake paid for the meal and he escorted me out of the restaurant. He pressed a few buttons on his phone and a limo arrived shortly after. As he opened up the door for me to go inside. He winked at me.

"I would love to see you tomorrow. Seeing you refreshes me after a long day."

I blushed again and nodded, not knowing what to say.

"You'll hear from me tomorrow. Have a blessed night, Miss Jahliyah." He then closed the door and we drove off. This was just the ending I needed after how the evening started. I was on cloud nine. Everything had been perfect. I reached into my purse and took out the taser. I then took out my cell phone and texted Shayla.

"This sugar baby thing is easy," I wrote.

A few minutes later, she replied, "It only goes up from here."

CHAPTER 6

I woke up the next morning, feeling giddy. The last week had been nothing short of amazing. I have never seen this type of treatment before. I felt like one of those reality TV show wives but I didn't have to deal with the disrespect or embarrassment. I got up and fixed myself a bowl of cereal. I had some thinking to do. I had officially used up all my sick days and vacation time. Was it wise to quit my job or should I do this full time?

I made more money in a week than I have in five months. Even if I wanted to quit in three weeks, I had enough to pay back Erica and get us out of the hood. I could always find another job. But I had a short window in being a sugar baby. I picked up my cell phone and dialed my DM. I told him that the commitments to my family were too much and that I had to resign immediately. He understood and wished me luck. I finished showering when I heard my text tone go off. It was Blake, asking me to meet him this afternoon. My luck was definitely changing.

It was an afternoon outing so I decided to go casual. With casual meaning a black and white Diane Von Furstenberg halter with red Rag and Bone skinny jeans. A Gucci clutch and matching Gloria shoes rounded everything up. I pulled my curls up into a top bun and slicked my lips with Fenty Lip Glow. A dash of mascara and highlighter completed my laid back look. I texted him that I was ready. I walked out of the house and locked the door behind me. Putting my hand on the taser, I walked with my head held high towards the limo that was pulling up in front of the parking lot of the projects. I got in the car and we drove off.

We drove to the Riverfront, where he was waiting for me. He was casually dressed in striped button up shirt and some fitted jeans. His Rolex gleamed in the sunlight. His tan skin glowed. He was so gorgeous. Too too gorgeous. He walked over to the car as I stepped out. He took my hand and kissed it. I felt my body tingle a little bit.

"Another day with one of the most beautiful women I

have ever laid eyes on. Come with me," he said as he led me down the dock and onto a small yacht. There were servants everywhere, preparing lobster, shrimp and steak in the kitchen. It was intoxicating. He led me to the deck to a small table with two chairs. Champagne was chilling in an ice bucket. It was so romantic.

"I normally would drive the boat myself, but I wanted to focus on you," he said as he pulled my chair out for me to sit. I sat down and he walked over to the other side of the table and sat across from me. He nodded towards the captain who steered the boat away from the dock and then we departed from National Harbor. I had never been on a boat before. It was really nice. Serene, quiet, but the differences in our lives were highlighted even more. It hurt me to think of all the struggles. I sighed.

"You may think that our lives are very different, but I think we have more in common than you think."

I turned to him. "What do you mean?"

"I am a lot older than you. In fact, I'm old enough to be your father."

I winced. He was right. He wasn't much younger than my father. The last time I saw my dad, I was almost thirteen years old. My dad was thirty five. That was almost seven years ago. He would be forty two now. Blake was thirty eight, almost twenty years older than me. I missed my parents. I fought back the tears, trying to maintain myself. I was a G; I wasn't a punk. I smiled.

"More experience and wisdom makes a man more interesting." I replied.

"Good save," he said, laughing. He winked at me and took my hand into his.

"There's a lot of division right now and frankly, DC is thriving on it. It's all a ruse, to keep everyone either in fear or entertained. There really isn't that much difference between us. Sure, there are more privileges given to certain people but we as a people have a lot more in common than you may think."

I was intrigued. "What do you mean?" I asked.

Blake poured us both a glass of wine. He took a sip before continuing, "Well, I grew up in a poor family. I know that white people poor and black people poor is different in the city but that's not where I'm from. I'm a rural, country boy. Mines was on some coal miner, Appalachian poor. We are good people but that's a poverty that most people have never experienced. Once I left high school, I had to work and save to go to college.

That took me forever because although I got a full ride academic scholarship to George Washington University, there were still some things that weren't covered, so it took me a while longer to get out. However, that was only for the first couple of years. I majored in business with a minor in political science.

I nodded my head, completely intrigued by his story. He continued,

"I graduated damn near top of my class. However, I couldn't get a job right out of undergrad because of the recession in the early 2000's, and I didn't want to return home where there was no opportunity for me. And although I interned at some very prestigious companies, I didn't have the clout or more specifically the connections to be hired or find something quickly, if you know what I mean."

The food arrived. Lobster tails with fingerling potatoes and asparagus. A small cup of lobster bisque completed the meal. We ate for a while before Blake continued with his story.

"I was unemployed for a while but I made do. Thank God I didn't have student loans or I would've been up shit's creek. It was about a year and half before I finally landed my dream job, working as an assistant campaign treasurer for a congressman. That led to me to working as a congressional aide and then starting my own political strategy company. And now here I am, one of the wealthiest men in DC, that isn't a politician."

That was an amazing story.

"So, tell me about you. What do you want to do?"

I didn't know who I was going to really answer that question. So I took a couple more bites of lobster tail and drank a small sip of wine before I spoke. I had to loosen myself up so that I wouldn't start crying.

"We have some things in common. I wasn't poor until..." I took a deep sigh and changed the subject. I felt the tears again. I took a deep breath and continued,

"I just know that I am motivated to want to change my life and find something better for me to do. I just don't know what that is because I never had the opportunity to explore my passions or find out what I wanted to do with myself. It's always been about surviving."

I shrugged my shoulders and looked at the condensation slowly drip down the side of my glass. Blake then stood up and pulled me towards him.

"Maybe now that you found me, you'll have the chance to relax and discover some of those things."

It was then that he gave me a soft kiss on the lips. I felt my body tingle.

"You should come away with me, so that you can discover those things and more." He kissed me again and I began to melt. I felt his hands run all over my body as he kissed me. I felt like I was being devoured by him when he suddenly broke the kiss. He pulled back from me.

"I should take you home."

I just nodded my head and pulled myself out of his lap. I sat back in my chair. Honestly, I didn't want to go home. I wanted to stay with Blake, but I had to respect what he said. Blake motioned for the captain to turn the ship around back to the port. It was now back to reality.

I arrived home about an hour and a half later to find Angie sitting in the living room waiting on me. Oh fuck, it was too early for her to be home. I was in for it.

"I've been hearing rumors, but I thought, not my Jahliyah. Her awkward ass is still a virgin as far as I know. So I had to see for myself, and right now you looking a little suspect."

I just stood there and listened to her rant. Angie continued,

"I take off my clothes for a living and I ain't fucking on no clients, so how you think I feel knowing my sister, who I do all this sacrificing for is out there, prostituting."

I took a deep breath. "Angie, I promise you that I'm not. There's always been that rumor about me and each time, it wasn't true. So why would I start now?"

"Because before you weren't bringing home Goyard Bags and Chanel jeans, that's why. That's why this time I believe what's being said."

"Angie, I swear, I'm not hoeing."

"Nigga, whatever. I don't even know what to say. I want to stomp the shit out of you right now for this shit."

"Do you what you need to do, but you gonna feel stupid when you find out that I'm not hoeing. In fact, let me show you."

I reached into my purse and showed Angie the card Shayla gave me. Angie snatched it from me and stared at it. She then looked back up at me.

"I'm a sugar baby and I don't have sex. My v-card still intact. I just give him companionship. That's it."

Angie continued to stare at me as my text tone went off. It was a message from Blake.

"Sometimes, we all need a place to start from," it said. I then received another alert from my bank saying I received a deposit. I logged into my account and there it was.

A deposit of ten thousand dollars.

More money in one time than I've ever had in my whole life...so far. I looked up at Angie. She was livid.

"I want you to stop."

"No," I said.

Angie was taken aback. "Excuse me?"

"I said no, Ang. Why is it okay for you to strip, but not okay for me to be a sugar baby?"

A tear slid down Angie's face. "Because you're special and you're supposed to be somebody." She then sat back down on the couch, defeated.

"Maybe Blake is going to help me figure that out. It would help if I also got paid in the time."

She looked up at me and shook her head. I continued,

Since you already know what's going on, I'm going to go away with Blake for a few days, to Los Angeles. But don't worry, I got you." I then transferred the money to Angie's linked account. Angie heard a buzz on her phone and checked it. She then looked back up at me.

"We should have a new apartment outside of the projects by the time I return." I then walked over and gave my sister a kiss on the forehead. She had nothing else to say to me. I then walked into my room. This was too much emotion for me for one day. I laid on my bed and went straight to sleep.

CHAPTER 7

The next day was filled with me packing and shopping for some new outfits for my trip with Blake. It felt so good to finally have the money to wear and have nice things. While on my excursion at Eight Twenty-Five, I also picked up a few things for Darryl and Angie. I had them dropped off to them. I didn't really want to have another showdown like I did with Angie the day before. After shopping, Blake had a limo take me to the address where he was waiting for me. On the car ride to the place, I couldn't help but think about how much my life has changed so much for the better in a matter of days. I didn't want this feeling to stop.

I never really had a crush before. I liked a few boys in my day, but they never showed interest back or it didn't really go anywhere. But this—this was different. I felt like all of them were just whatever. And I thought that Blake may be my first real crush. I knew it wasn't love because it was too soon. We just met and Shayla made me promise not to do that. But I'll admit, it was getting kind of tough, but as Three Stacks said, keep your heart. I intended to do just that. We finally arrived at the address. When I got out of the car it was then I realized that it was a landing strip.

Blake was taking me on a private jet. I was so excited that I couldn't help but pull out my phone and take a picture. I immediately sent it to Shayla. Blake was waiting for me at the plane near the bottom of the stairs.

"You look beautiful as always. I really do appreciate the time you take to look nice for me. My wife doesn't do that."

I was briefly taken aback at him mentioning his wife.

"Shall we?" he said as he took my hand and led me up the stairs into the jet. As we sat down and were read the flight instructions, Blake winked and squeezed my hand. Shortly afterwards, we were taking off.

I watched as DC disappeared into the clouds. It was truly a breathtaking sight. While on the four-hour flight, we drank champagne and ate lunch.

"I never been to L.A. before," I said to him.

"I've been plenty of times but only for business. However, since this is your first time, I will make sure to show you some of the sights. But L.A is not the final destination. From there, we will be going to Miami and then to Aspen."

I looked up at him in surprise. "I didn't bring enough clothes."

Blake laughed. "Not to worry because we'll go shopping."

I smiled at him. He then leaned in to kiss me again. The kiss took my breath away. All time stopped and I felt lightheaded. I was beginning to have thoughts, of doing something that I had planned never to do, which was have sex with Blake. But the way he made my body tingle, I just couldn't help myself. It was my first time, but I didn't want to tell him that. I just didn't want to seem like I was a rookie. So I let him take the lead. His mouth felt amazing as his tongue caressed my neck and made its way underneath my top. The boys that I allowed to kiss me before never made me feel this way. They were always in a rush. However, with Blake he took his time as if he savored the very essence of me. I wanted to pull back but when I felt his tongue snake around my nipple, I was done for. And I let him take me to the King.

I was always told that sex with white men was wack as fuck. They weren't packing like the brothers, but with Blake that was simply not true. My first time was amazing. He was very loving and gentle. He kissed and licked me all over, making a trail with his tongue down my nani. He swirled his tongue around my clit and gently sucked it between his lips. I wanted to cry out but I didn't because I didn't want to alert the staff. So I grabbed his head and grinded my hips against his mouth. I was just about to arrive when he stopped and looked at me. I knew it was time to reciprocate. I didn't know what to do but instinct took over.

I reached down to pull him out of his boxers and go down on him but he stopped me. Putting his finger to my lips, he gently pushed me back down in the seat and then slowly parted my lips, entering me. They said that the first time would hurt. It did feel a little weird being filled up. He was thick and hard. I felt every inch of him, and although this was my first time, I knew it was a large one. He then started to move back and forth and my body radiated and tingled. I relaxed a little bit more and enjoyed him. Blake leaned over me and started driving himself deeper inside of me. He threw his head back as I sunk my nails into his shoulders, his mouth open and breathing hard. I bit my lower lip as I took him.

I felt this feeling start to build up in me as if I was on a gently rocking boat that was about to capsize. However, just before I was about to be taken overboard, I felt Blake slowly pull out of me with a groan. He looked down at his dick and his eyes widened in surprised. He then looked at me. I smiled at him, guiltily. He then reached over and wiped himself off. There was blood all over him.

"Were you on your period?" he asked me.

I looked down, embarrassed, and shook my head no. He then nodded knowingly and bit his lower lip. Blake then leaned over and kissed me gently on top of my forehead. He sat down on the chair across from me, smiling but in his eyes I could tell that he didn't know what to say or do. We got dressed. As we landed, he reached over and grabbed my hand. The deed was done and there was no going back.

After we landed and left the private airstrip, another limo arrived and whisked away to a large, country resort. After check in, we were escorted to a penthouse suite. The place was huge, beautiful with a view of the Pacific Ocean. I walked into the bathroom to fully clean up.

The bathroom alone was literally the size of my entire apartment in the projects. And we lived in one of the larger ones. I took out my phone and snapped another photo, sending it to Shayla. My text tone dinged again. It was Angie.

"I'm sorry that I snapped at you the way I did. I am being a hypocrite. Sometimes, when there is nothing else to offer, our bodies are the only things that can keep us moving, both literally and figuratively. I just want better for you. Just be careful out there. I don't want you to end up on a milk carton."

I smiled and texted back. "I want better for you too, but whatever you do, DON'T TELL DARRYL!!!111"

"Where are you?" she responded.

"I'm in Los Angeles, but we have a few other pit stops to make before I come back to DC. Check this out." I sent her a photo of the penthouse. She texted back,

"Just keep me posted. I love you."

"I love you, too," I replied.

"Before we go, I gotta know, did you FUCK him?"

My heart sank. I hated lying to my sister. "No. I'm still intact."

That was the last thing I said to her. I sat down on the toilet and wiped the small trickles of blood that came out. My v-card was gone, but at least it was given to someone that made sure I was taken care of. Many females can't say that. I hated justifying things. I sighed and washed my hands. I walked out of the penthouse to be greeted by several people. Blake came out of the bedroom and handed me a beautiful coral-colored dress. I looked at the tag: OSCAR DE LA RENTA. This man.....

"I didn't know what to say. If I had've known, I would have made it way more special because you deserve that. I..." He placed his hand over his face, rubbing his chin. "I will make it up to you with dinner tonight. But for now, I hope this helps."

I just smiled at him. He winked at me and kissed me on the forehead.

"I hate to leave you, but I have to go do a work check-in. I will be back as soon as I can." He gave me another kiss on the lips and left, shutting the door behind him. The staff asked me several questions at once.

"Would you like a massage?"

"How would you like your hair?

"Per the occasion?" One man said while eyeing my gown, "Do you want a natural look or a more sexy look?"

I was suddenly overwhelmed. "Excuse me," I said as I made my way to the bathroom. I sat down on the toilet with my head in my hands. Everything was moving so fast and I didn't know what to do. I looked at my phone and texted Shayla. I needed some advice. After a few moments of waiting, her only reply to me was,

"Calm down and have fun."

Easy for her to say, I thought. I received another alert on my phone. $20,000 had just been transferred to my bank account. I needed to get my shit together. I had a family to take care of. Let's get this show started, I said to myself, and walked out of the bathroom.

A few hours later, I was thoroughly relaxed and dressed for dinner. The dress fit me perfectly. The stylist gave me barrel curls that cascaded over one side of my shoulder. My makeup was a soft smoky eye with highlighter and nude lip-gloss. I looked absolutely stunning. When I greeted Blake in the limo, he just stared at me for a moment before helping me inside the car. I turned to him.

"I just wanted to thank you for your..."

He interrupted and helped me get inside of the car. He closed the door and got back inside. Shortly after the car pulled off. We rode in silence for a few moments, and then he spoke.

I don't want to talk about it, but that part of our relationship is just a formality. I'd rather act like it doesn't exist, especially since I really like being around you."

I just nodded my head. He continued,

"I know I'm married and that may be off putting, especially since I took your virginity."

I lowered my head and nodded, ashamed.

"But do understand that my wife is only for show and not for love. Truth is, I've been a client with the agency trying to find someone who I can love, and you're the first woman I've met who seems to fit. I didn't mean to take advantage of you and I don't want you to feel like less than because I'm married. I think about you all of the time and want to get to know you more."

I was shocked. "You do?"

He leaned over and kissed me, "I do." I felt the front of my dress fall away from me, exposing my bra. I felt his tongue trace a path from lip, to my neck, to my nipples. I threw my head back as I grabbed his head. His hands snaked up my leg where he found my nani and began to rub. I instantly became wet.

"Good girl," he said before he started kissing me again. "I need a quick one before dinner. I promise to be gentle."

I nodded my head as he pulled aside my underwear and unbuckled his pants. He groaned slightly as he entered me. The position felt crazy. I was slightly sitting up and he was in front of me, holding down my hips and he moved back and forth. He leaned over me, trying to get as deep inside of me as he could. It still felt amazing and didn't hurt one bit. Maybe I was made for this man. I bit my lower lip and held on to the back of the seat as my body began to melt. I couldn't hold it back anymore. I screamed as I arrived. Immediately, Blake laughed and put his hand over my mouth. His face went dreamy as he felt me shake and melt all over him. He then pulled out of me and sat next to me, breathless. A few moments later, we were at our destination. By the time the driver stopped the car, we regrouped and were dressed as if nothing happened.

It was an awards gala for one of the California caucuses. I must have met at least eighty different people.

Everyone knew who he was. It was a bit overwhelming, but it felt awesome to be with someone who commanded so much power and respect. There were no side eyes or anything. Everyone was so nice and intelligent and tried to include me in their conversations. Thanks to all of my training I was able to hold my own. As we sat at the party, I couldn't help but think about how well I fit into this life. It was like living in another world for me. I never wanted to go back to what I left. I also had to get Angie out of there too.

When we returned for the party, I took off all of my makeup and prepared myself for bed. Blake watched me and smiled.

"You are even more beautiful without all of that on."

I turned to him and smiled.

"If you would feel more comfortable, we could sleep in separate rooms. I don't want you to assume anything." My heart sank a little bit and I didn't know exactly what to do.

"But I will let you follow your heart," he said and left the room. I had already made my decision. I pinned up my hair and wrapped it up with a silk scarf. He would just have to get used to how I was going to do things. I got up and turned off the light in the bathroom. I walked over and I crept in there slowly, as to not disturb.

I got into bed.

I felt warm.

His warmth.

I was where I truly belonged.

CHAPTER 8

The next few weeks we just travelled, shopped and made love. While Blake was at work, he would leave me a stack of money to do what I wished. I wanted to go to the bank and just deposit it all, but I didn't want to seem suspicious. So I made sure to spend lavishly at the famous shopping destinations of each city we visited. When in Los Angeles, I made my home at the Cartier store on Rodeo Drive. After a week, we flew down to Miami. White sand beaches, clear turquoise water and beautiful, tan skin. Although it was all the Atlantic Ocean, the water, the atmosphere, everything was just better here. When Blake was away, I walked around South Beach, taking in the sights. Although it was going towards winter, the weather was a super warm 85 degrees. Up in DC, it was probably 50 degrees but felt like it was 45 because of wind-chill. Needless to say, I wasn't missing that.

Blake was always so extra, making sure that every whim I had was catered to. This must have been what it was like to be the queen of a country. It was all so over-whelming. However, down in Miami, Blake was more subdued, down to earth. He definitely treated me to nice things, such as tearing up the stores in South Beach; however, the way he spent time with me was different. In LA, it was one gala or party or meeting after the next, with each one requiring a different dress and a different conversation. It was proving to be exhausting.

Miami showed me a different side of Blake. A more human side, so to speak. He was always on whenever we were out. Wheeling and dealing, making moves. I wanted him to relax and Miami gave me that wish. He took me to Little Haiti and Little Havana, to the real Miami, not the touristy areas that you saw on the videos and in magazines. And of course, he knew everyone and everyone knew him. Each day brought us a different flavor of the city. In Little Haiti, we ate diri ak pwa wouj with griyot and French soda. When in little Havana we ate arroz con pollo. I never tasted such delicious food in my life. It was all so new to me. Growing up, we ate Jamaican food, but that was when my life was normal.

Once we were dropped off to live at my aunt's house, we were lucky if we even ate.

He was fascinated with Black Cuban culture He would converse with the locals in their native language and save from looking at them, you wouldn't know who was talking to who. He sounded so natural. That day he took me to a priestess.

"What are we here for?" I asked, while looking at around the different statues and altars.

He winked at me. "Wouldn't you like to know?"

"You don't need any of this stuff to get me. I'm already yours."

He smiled at me. "Good to know. I just came in here to look around. I don't get too much off time where I can just enjoy myself. So now that I finished up my assignment for the week and I'm here with the most beautiful woman in the world, I thought to myself, sightsee, be a tourist for once." He took my hand and pulled me towards him. I melted.

We finished the day at a small family-owned Cuban restaurant, dining on ropa vieja and moro. The place was by the beach with a dancefloor that led directly to the sand. There was live band playing salsa and merengue music in the background. We watched the sky turn pink as the sun began to move to the west. I turned back to Blake and smiled. The night truly was perfect. I was beginning to think that I went through hell so that I could truly appreciate the heavens that were waiting for me. I knew to never take anything for granted and I was grateful for everything that was given to me. Blake stared at me with a slight grin on his face. He stood up and took my hand.

"Dance with me."

He pulled me up out of the chair and led me to the dance floor.

"I don't know how to dance salsa," I said, trying not to stumble. I was full of sangria and I was starting to feel the effects.

"Just follow my lead," he said.

I smiled. "I'll follow you anywhere."

We danced. My step with his. Letting him lead me into ecstasy. Under the moonlight in Miami. We didn't get home until one in the morning.

We left the following day to Aspen, where because of the weather, I felt a little bit more at home. I slept the entire three and half hour flight to Colorado, still intoxicated from the night before. I wasn't sure if it was the sangria or Blake that had me in such a state. Blake was able to work from the cabin that he rented for us. Colorado was more scenic, with snow-capped mountains everywhere. Like a true white winter wonderland. I lounged around most days while Blake conducted his conference calls and wrote campaign plans for his clients. He was preparing for the special elections and for the 2018 preliminary elections. It seemed all so interesting, watching how our government really worked from behind the scenes.

Around 11 AM on a Wednesday, after we had been here for a few days, Blake ended one of his phone calls and walked over to the balcony, where I was sitting, sipping on a mug of hot chocolate. He kissed me on the shoulder and stood in front of me, grabbing my hand.

"Let's hit the slopes," he said.

"What?"

"Let's go skiing."

He pulled me up out of my seat and led me into the bedroom, where I found snow gear in just my size laying on the bed.

"I've never been skiing before."

"Well," he said, smiling. "First time for everything."

We were soon suited and dressed in our ski suits. We headed down to the main cabin where our ski instructor was waiting for us. Blake turned to me and asked,

"Which one would you like to learn? Snowboarding or skiing?"

I couldn't make a decision at the moment. I knew how to skateboard so snowboarding would probably be similar.

"How about we do both?" Blake said, smiling.

"Bet," I answered.

He took us to a beginner's slope where we both strapped on our skis. As always while I was stumbling and falling, Blake was there, laughing and taking photos of me.

"You better not post those."

"No, these are for my private collections."

"Whatever," I said as I got up.

We then switched over and went to the intermediate slope for our snowboarding lesson. I did a little bit better with this because of skateboarding; however, Blake, as with everything else that he did in life, commanded the slope. I watched him in awe as he flipped down the mountainside. My instructor smiled at me and said,

"He's still got it."

I turned to him. "What do you mean, he still got it?"

"Oh, you don't know?"

I looked at him in awe. "No."

"Blake Austin was one of the first X-game snowboarders. A legend."

My eyebrow raised. This man never ceased to amaze me. "He is a legend, alright."

We finally returned to our cabin at around 4 pm. We were greeted with fresh lobster, Waldorf salad and cauliflower mash with sautéed asparagus as the sides. We freshened up and sat down across from each other. He lit the two candles in front of us and prepared two mimosas. We ate in silence for a few moments before I decided to bring up what I heard at practice.

"Soo.... X-games?" I said, blinking hard.

Blake almost spit out his mimosa, laughing. "Who told you that?"

"Our ski instructor. I mean I know that you're the best at everything, but the X-games also. You are something else."

He laughed again. "I didn't exactly lie to you. Remember when I said that college was paid for but I still had to take some jobs to make ends meet/ That's what I meant."

"That's not some little job."

"No job is better than the other. It got me where I needed to go and that's it."

"You never cease to amaze me," I said in awe.

"You never cease to amaze me as well."

I blushed.

I walked back out onto the balcony and sat down with a mug of hot cocoa. I looked at my phone and decided to text Angie. I had been texting her on and off the whole time I'd been on vacation. I had been sending her half the money that I was making also. I wanted her to find a new apartment, preferably at Eight Twenty Five or something similar. I had made enough to finance our apartment for a year. In our discussions, Angie told me she found a great apartment, one that was near the heart of DC. We would be safe there. She contacted some movers but I told her to only pack up our stuff and to get rid of all the furniture. She could get one of the fully furnished ones. I really didn't want any remnants of our old life.

I picked up my phone and texted her.

"Hey booski. Will everything be squared away by the time I come back?"

"Are you coming back?" she texted shortly after.

"Of course I am," I replied.

"Well you might be disappointed."

"That's nothing new."

"But you sure are acting like it."

I wanted to call her, but I didn't want to alarm Blake if we started yelling, so I kept texting her. "What is that supposed to mean?"

"Things just don't happen because you throw money around. I'm still the big sister and your money won't allow you to talk out the side of your neck to me."

"I'm not talking disrespectfully to you at all, Angie. I

just want you to stop stripping, stop doing all that shit. I'm scared for you every night."

"I'm not going to stop stripping. Not until I have a job that can sustain me outside of stripping that will pay me what I make taking off my clothes. I'm not here to rely on you, Jae or whatever money you're getting, because nothing is guaranteed. EVER."

"I know and that is why I'm trying my best to maximize what I can."

"Look, I gotta go, Jae. Check in with me later."

I just looked at my phone, not knowing what to say. I hated arguing with Angie. I felt something warm in back of me and then a small cold chain being buckled behind my neck. I looked down and saw the Panthere De Cartier gold, onyx and diamond necklace. My heart stopped. This necklace was at least 70,000 dollars. More money than I had ever seen in my life.

"I heard some furious typing there. Your sister loves you, and she's just concerned. Let her be your big sister."

I looked up and nodded my head. I smiled at him. The troubles with Angie slowly faded away.

CHAPTER 9

We returned back to DC on the private jet. He decided to ride home with me in the limo. Unfortunately, it was still the same projects that I'd been in for the last half of my life. I just didn't want him to go there and see all of the depression. I didn't want our excursion to end.

"Jae?"

"Yes?" I responded.

"Is it okay if we continue seeing each other?" Blake asked me.

Excited, I smiled. "Yes, of course we can. I also wanted to thank you him for your generosity. For everything. This was truly amazing. I never knew life could be like this."

"It can be that way and more. Before I take you home, Jae, can we stop by my house?"

"Sure."

We drove the rest of the way to his house, hand in hand. Once, we stopped and the door opened to the Totten Mews, one of the most exclusive communities in DC. I sat in the car and stared out the open door as Blake walked around the car and towards his porch. Blake looked back at me and smiled.

"It's okay for you to come inside," he said as he winked at me. I got out of the car and walked behind him. He opened the door and I walked in front of him.

The place was spectacular. It was an open air design. Everything was just... opulent, a sign of true wealth. I didn't even want to fully walk inside. I was scared to. Placing his hand on the small of my back, he lightly pushed me inside so he could close the door behind him. The furniture was modern, glossy, white with splashes of bright colors everywhere. The walls were dark shades of blue, red and green making a striking contrast against the white decor. Expensive artwork decorated the walls; however, one in particular, hung over the fireplace, made my heart twist and ache, my stomach churning.

It was a picture of Blake and his wife over the mantel. If the painting was any indication of how his wife looked, she was very beautiful. I didn't know why Blake had a hard time connecting with her. I put it out of my mind. I couldn't feel bad about this. I couldn't. There was something wrong. Not everything that looks good on the outside actually is, I reasoned with myself. If this woman couldn't keep Blake happy, then I would.

My text tone rang. It was Angie, giving me the address to the new apartment. She lied. It was Eight Twenty-Five. Dreams do come true.

Blake walked up to me and gave me a kiss on the forehead.

"This is where I bid you adieu. I have a car, waiting for you. I will see you soon."

I was riding in the limo, anticipating my new apartment. When I walked up to my new place, the movers were still bringing in some of our items. I almost wanted to cry. I was so excited and thankful to no longer be in the projects. Until I realized that there was no sign of Angie. I went into our rooms. She wasn't anywhere to be found. I was getting angry. I was about to call her when I heard the door open behind me. Angie walked into the apartment and the happiness of seeing my sister overwhelmed me. She didn't seem as eager to see me though. I ran up to her and gave her a tight hug. She smiled at me.

"Hood rule number one. Never leave no niggas in your house unattended. Where are you coming from?"

"We aren't in the hood anymore. You were so eager to leave. And I just left our aunt's house," she said.

I was incensed. "You better not have given that hoodrat any of my money."

"I didn't. I gave her some of MY money. I just can't let her starve and die, Jae."

"I don't agree with you on that shit at all. Especially after all the shit that she's done to us since dad left. But I'm going to leave it alone because I just want to be happy."

"I want to also," Angie replied. She hugged me again. "I love our new place."

"I do too."

Once the movers were finished, I looked around our new apartment. It was beautiful. This was the way life should be lived. I took out my phone and took some pictures. I sent the pictures to Darryl. This was the first time that I had contacted him in a couple weeks. I honestly had been avoiding him, because of everything that was going on, but I needed to talk to my best friend. He responded shortly after.

"What you do to get all of this?"

"Angie. All Angie."

"Shit, maybe I need to strip."

I laughed. "I would throw a couple dollars your way," I responded. I just couldn't face telling Darryl the truth. He used to make fun of girls like me. I knew I would have to tell him eventually because if he found out from someone else, he may stop being friends with me. And that would devastate me.

I loved Darryl. He and Angie were all I had. No matter how much money came my way, those were the two that mattered. And I would hold on to them at all costs.

CHAPTER 10

The next day I met up with Shayla for lunch. She stared at me in awe as I sat down across from her. She smiled at me.

"Girllll, you look like money. And a lot of it. How are things with you and Blake?"

"Going well. He wants to continue to see me."

"Girl, jackpot. I love it. Having one steady, regular customer is better than having two or three who only call you sometimes. It's the lean months that can make things difficult. But when you have a main one, it's almost like having a full time job and the benefits are definitely better."

"I do have a confession to make." I said, "I started sleeping with Blake."

"Girlll... Is he good?"

I looked down at the menu.

"Good girl. Don't tell anyone anything like that. It doesn't matter that you sleeping with him. One of the perks of the job if you ask me; however, please be careful not to fall for him. From those few texts and even the way you looked when you mention his name, it seems like you are."

"I'm not. I'm in love with the lifestyle and what he gives me."

"That's how it should be," Shayla responded.

After lunch was over, I decided to go over to meet with Erica. We were supposed to check in with her each time we came back from one of our vacations. I walked into Erica's office and she was all smiles as I sat across from her.

"Blake shared the great news that you guys are working out really well. He really enjoys your company and wants to work with you solely. That is amazing considering that he was known as one of our more difficult, well I like to call it, discerning clients. I knew you were special, but you must be a miracle worker."

"No. Your classes just refined me."

"I see," Erica said, smiling, "Since you're able to do the impossible, I was wondering how you would feel about taking on new clients."

My heart sank. I couldn't do that. I couldn't spread myself so thin. I had to think of something. "I can't." I said, "I'm still getting the hang of things and wants to keep it at just Blake for the time being." Deep down, I had feelings for Blake and honestly felt like I would be cheating on him if I started dating other people. What if it was someone who knew him or ran in his circles? I just couldn't do it.

Erica gave me the onceover. "Are you sure? There's more money to be made."

I swallowed hard and nodded my head. "I will take on more clients once I'm more settled." However I knew that day would probably never come.

Over the course of the next month, Blake and I saw each other regularly, sometimes three or four times in a week. We explored every bit of DC together, with quite a few excursion to New York, Philadelphia and Virginia. And each Saturday morning, like clockwork, I would wake up to a $10,000 deposit in my account. However, I didn't set foot in his house again since that first time. I didn't mind though. I just didn't feel right being in another woman's home.

Blake and I had gotten closer than I ever was with anyone else. I still didn't let him know too much about me, with my dad and mom. I didn't think I would ever let anyone really know about that, but in everything else I was free. We made love everywhere and he made my body feel things that I never thought were possible. I began to crave him, not because of the money, but for everything that he was. Powerful, handsome, gentle, loving and strong. I just didn't really understand how any woman could not go out of her way to please him. While inside the limo, waiting to go on another excursion, I received a text inviting me to spend the weekend at his home. I felt uncomfortable but who was I to tell him no. I had to respect his wishes. All of them.

It was the last part of winter going towards spring, so I was able to dress a little bit lighter than before. I decided to get sexy by wearing just a heavy trench coat and lingerie. The limo pulled up to his townhome and there he was waiting for me at the door. I walked out in my Louboutin heels, Burberry Trench and Agent Provocateur lingerie. I made my way through the open door and into his home. The fireplace was blazing and there were two glasses of champagne glistening on ice near the rug. As I walked over to the fireplace, I felt him unbuckle my trench from behind and pull the coat away from my shoulders. He turned me around and licked his lips before pulling me into a passionate kiss.

"I missed you," were the only words that escaped from his mouth before he pulled me down to the floor. The heat from the fireplace warmed my skin as he laid me down and picked up one of the champagne glasses. With his other hand, he pulled off all of my clothes and threw them to the side. He looked at me hungrily, his blue eyes glowing in the firelight.

My God he was sexy.

He slowly poured champagne all over my body. The coolness in contrast to the heat of the fire, made my nipples hard and my nani wet. I was ready and waiting for him. The champagne fizzed all over my body as he lowered his head and began to lick up every drop from my nipples, to my stomach and down to the sweet spot. I loved it when he went down. As he kissed and sucked my little pearl, I grabbed his hair. I threw my head back as I climaxed, letting the waves of heat and lust wash all over me. He kissed his way back up my body while slowly entered me. Taking my hips in one of his hands and pressing down on my pelvis with the other, he sat back up and began to long stroke me, making sure his shaft found every inch of my clit. I grabbed at the rug on the floor as I came over and over again. After what must have been my fifth climax, he finally allowed himself to release, pulling out of me, spilling his seeds on the floor.

He laid next to me, completely spent, the fire highlighting the contours and crevasses of his muscles. He smiled at me as he closed his eyes. I was truly happy. My life had changed so much for the better and it was all because of this man. I may have been actually falling in love with him. It was easy to admit to myself, harder to admit to others, although Shayla suspected it and even Erica could probably see it. It was hard not to fall in love with him. He was everything that any woman, black, white and everything in between could want. I felt myself getting drowsy. I pulled one of the throws off of the couch and fell asleep.

I woke up the next morning to a gentle kiss on the lips.

"Shower time, my dear."

I nodded my head and got up. Taking my hand, he led me upstairs to their bathroom. I looked around in awe. The bathroom was literally the size of my old apartment. He walked over to the glass shower and turned it on. It had two large shower heads with detachable parts that were located on opposite ends of the shower. I was so ready for this. I tied up my hair before we got inside. He began to slowly lather me up before turning me around and swirling his tongue around my nipples.

This man really knew how to get to me. Before I could fully enjoy his tongue on my body, he turned me around and bent me over. I gripped the sides of the shower as he roughly entered me from behind, moving in and out of me as his left hand reached between my thighs and rubbed my clit. I couldn't move at all. I didn't want to. I was a prisoner to the pleasure that he gave me. I moaned softly with each stroke in and out of my body. I heard his soft groans of pleasure as he felt my walls grip him. It was steamy inside, with no sounds but the shower, my cries of pleasure and his moans of ecstasy which didn't seem so out of place. However, what was startling was the sound of the bathroom door opening...

And there she stood...

The woman from the painting...

In all of her glory...

Walking in on her husband, fucking another woman in her home... In her shower.

We were caught, red handed...

And didn't know what to do.

FIND out what happens next in Secrets Of A Sugar Baby Book 2! Available Now!

FOLLOW Mia Black on Instagram for more updates: @authormiablack

SECRETS OF A SUGAR BABY 2

Becoming a sugar baby turns out to be a lot easier than Jae thinks, but no sooner does she start to get her money up, she finds herself in a new set of trouble. Jae gets caught up in a love triangle with her sponsor, Blake, and her childhood crush, Darryl.

Now Jae has a really big problem—one she didn't anticipate and one that could change everything if she makes the wrong move.

Find out what happens in part two of Secrets Of A Sugar Baby!

To find out when Mia Black has new books available, **follow Mia Black on Instagram: @authormiablack**

www.ingramcontent.com/pod-product-compliance
Lightning Source LLC
Chambersburg PA
CBHW071343150726
47997CB00002B/846